PUFFIN BOOKS

CHRIS AND THE DRAGON

Chris Chudley is always getting into trouble. It starts with the brightly lit Christmas dragon display on the town roundabout, where Chris trips over a wire and causes an explosion! Unluckily for Chris, Mrs Maltby the headmistress just happens to be passing at the time.

After that, Chris makes a big effort to be good, especially when he's picked for the part of Joseph in the school nativity play. And, apart from a few slips, he manages to keep out of trouble with Mrs Maltby up to the very last moment . . .

But perhaps the funniest episode in this lively story is the school's Chinese New Year celebration, when Mrs Maltby surprises everybody by her unexpected and startling behaviour!

Fay Sampson is a part-time teacher in mathematics and lecturer in writing. She has written several children's books and in the course of writing has found herself learning Welsh, horse-riding and sailing, and studying archaeology. She is married with two grown-up children and lives in Devon.

'A compulsive story' – *Books for Your Children*, 1986

CHRIS
AND THE DRAGON

Fay Sampson

Illustrated by Jill Bennett

PUFFIN BOOKS

PUFFIN BOOKS

Published by the Penguin Group
Penguin Books Ltd, 27 Wrights Lane, London W8 5TZ, England
Penguin Books USA Inc., 375 Hudson Street, New York, New York 10014, USA
Penguin Books Australia Ltd, Ringwood, Victoria, Australia
Penguin Books Canada Ltd, 2801 John Street, Markham, Ontario, Canada L3R 1B4
Penguin Books (NZ) Ltd, 182–190 Wairau Road, Auckland 10, New Zealand

Penguin Books Ltd, Registered Offices: Harmondsworth, Middlesex, England

First published by Victor Gollancz Ltd 1985
Published in Puffin Books 1987
3 5 7 9 10 8 6 4 2

Copyright © Fay Sampson, 1985
Illustrations copyright © Jill Bennett, 1985
All rights reserved

Printed in England by Clays Ltd, St Ives plc
Typeset in Bembo

For David

Contents

1

The Roundabout

It was a dark, wintry day, and raining. But already the Christmas decorations were going up. Chris and Steve, on their way home from school, dodged through the crowds of shoppers. They had their hoods pulled over their heads. Santa Claus beamed at them as they hurried past. Big windows, full of presents, had been edged with white to look like frost. Christmas trees sprouted above shop doorways.

Chris tripped over a pushchair.

"Watch your steering!" he growled at the baby.

Then he grabbed Steve's arm.

"Look! They're putting the lights up!"

All along Blackwell Street hung a net of multi-coloured light bulbs, still unlit. Silver stars were suspended from it, so low that they almost scraped the tops of the double-decker buses.

Steve swung round. They were both thinking the same.

"The roundabout! What have they done this year?"

They began to run, bumping against shopping bags. Their soggy shoes spattered through the puddles.

The roundabout at the top of Blackwell Street was no ordinary traffic island. It was not just a circle of concrete and grass. Even in summer it was special. It was a huge mound, like an island in a storybook. Real trees grew on it. Huge boulders had been piled there, with clefts between them like dark caves. Anything could happen on it. Especially at Christmas.

"Last year it was a castle. Knights on horses and a drawbridge." Words pumped out of Chris as he pounded in front of Steve.

"Remember when they did that Viking ship? All those shields and battleaxes? That was terrific."

They were almost at the top of Blackwell Street. Chris turned round and Steve bumped into him.

"Shut your eyes," ordered Chris. "Now. Guess."

"A Wild West fort? With Apaches?"

"A space rocket. And bug-eyed monsters!" Then Chris groaned. His eyes were still tight shut. "I bet they haven't. It'll be one of their economy cuts. I bet they haven't decorated the roundabout this year."

But even as he spoke there was a gasp all around them. Their eyes flew open. All down the length of the street the coloured lights had come on, like a roof of jewels. And there in front of them, on the roundabout, blazed a Chinese palace. Four high golden walls surrounded it. Above them, pale in the floodlights, rose a real weeping willow tree. Inside the walls, on the very summit, a pagoda soared. Turret after turret climbed towards the dark sky, each sweeping scarlet roof smaller than the one beneath it. On the highest pinnacle was a peacock, with coloured light bulbs in its tail.

But the best of all, around the edge of the traffic island, one at each compass point, crouched four great dragons. They glowed from inside with a weird emerald light. Their red eyes sparkled.

"Magic!" breathed Steve.

"Fantastic!" shouted Chris.

They leaned on the railings at the edge of the pavement. Their imaginations were racing.

"There must be treasure inside that pagoda," declared Steve. "Those dragons are guarding it."

"And between us and them there's a dangerous sea. Can you see all them man-eating sharks?"

The wet and shining cars hissed past them. Their

11

headlights circled the island like pairs of hungry eyes.

Chris and Steve looked at each other. A grin spread over both their faces. They had forgotten the rain.

"Are you thinking what I'm thinking? Let's find the treasure!"

They waited for a gap in the traffic, then dashed across and on to the mound.

"Round one to us. The sharks didn't get us," gasped Chris, climbing on to a rock.

From here, the lighted shop-fronts looked far away. A sodden tree shivered above them and a shower of raindrops trickled down their necks. The nearest dragon glowed with an unearthly green light.

"What now?" whispered Steve.

"Kill that dragon, of course," Chris breathed.

They stole towards it over the steep, squelching grass. When they got near, they could see that the dragon was made of fibreglass, hollow inside. Black cables snaked into it through a large hole at the back.

"It's only wires and light bulbs," said Chris, disappointed.

"Those are its veins," Steve told him. "They're full of deadly poison. If you stab it and the blood spurts over you, you die in agony."

"You would too," observed Chris, stepping over

13

them carefully. "They must be carrying at least a thousand volts."

"How do we kill it then?"

"Strangle it with our bare hands. You first."

The dragon beside them gave a low roar.

"Yow!" shrieked Steve, and stumbled into Chris, who sat down heavily with Steve on top of him. They scrambled to their feet. Chris's trousers were plastered with mud.

"It roared!" squeaked Steve. "That dragon roared."

"Couldn't have," said Chris. "They pay the Electricity Board to light it up, not to do sound effects as well."

The dragon roared again. Quietly, but quite definitely. It seemed to be watching them with its nearest red eye.

Chris shook Steve by the hand.

"Well, it's been nice knowing you, mate. If I go up in a puff of smoke, look for my latch-key and take it back to my old Mum."

He went down on his hands and knees and crawled through the hole at the back of the dragon.

The inside was a green cave. It was blazing with light bulbs. Chris squinted upwards. There was someone else already there. He was laughing. It was Tuan, the Chinese boy from Vietnam. He was the smallest boy in Chris's class, with the smallest voice. Chris blinked in astonishment.

"That was *you*? You made it roar like that?"

Tuan nodded. His brown eyes were dancing.

"Yes. Do you want to try? You put your head through the mouth like this. Grrr!"

Tuan's roar was quite a small one, but it echoed hollowly through the opening. Chris thought of Steve, alone in the rain.

"Let me have a go!"

Chris was taller than Tuan. There was hardly room for him to stand up. The dragon rocked dangerously as he pushed past Tuan and leaned

15

through the neck of the dragon.

"GRRR!"

His roar was much louder. A woman on the pavement opposite dropped her shopping bag and clutched at her friend. They looked all round them in fright. Then they hurried on.

There was a scuffle behind the boys. Steve squeezed his way in.

"You rotten beast! You might have told me. I nearly died of heart failure. I've probably got pneumonia anyway."

Chris roared again. Steve peered out through one of the red eyes. He saw a policeman riding a bicycle wobble sharply.

"It's great! Let me!" cried Steve.

But he was laughing so much that all that came out was a loud explosion, like a dragon's sneeze.

The policeman braked, got off his bicycle and took his helmet off. They watched him shake it upside down, then shake his head as well. He put his helmet back on and stood listening. The boys clutched each other, laughing hysterically.

"It's a real Chinese dragon!" gasped Tuan. "I didn't expect to find one in England."

"And it eats policemen!" cried Chris, roaring again.

16

Steve had gone back to the red window that was the dragon's eye.

"Oh-oh! I don't want to worry you," he said, "but I've just spotted an English dragon and it's coming this way."

A grey-haired woman in a white raincoat was crossing the pavement towards her car. At Chris's roar she stopped and stared straight at the dragon. It was Mrs Maltby, their headmistress.

"CRUMBS!" yelled Chris. "MRS MALTBY!"

The name roared across the road through the dragon's mouth.

An expression of fury crossed the headmistress's face. She thrust her car keys back in her pocket and began to march across the road towards the traffic island. Chris backed out of the dragon's neck, horrified.

"Help! She'll fry me alive!"

"Scarper!" cried Steve. He was down on his knees, scuttling out through the hole.

Tuan went next. They were racing through the dark bushes towards the golden pagoda. Chris plunged after them. His toe caught in an unseen cable. Behind him there was a fizzing explosion and a flash of brilliant blue sparks. The dragon went lifeless and dark.

Chris leaped away from the live cable, his heart thudding. There was a screech of brakes around the traffic island. One car hit the bumper in front of it. He heard glass shatter. The policeman shouted.

"Chris! Quick!" called Tuan.

He sprinted after them, in through the door in the wall surrounding the golden pagoda.

It was dark and still inside the four high walls. The floodlights were pointed high above their heads at the climbing scarlet roofs of the pagoda.

"What now?" panted Steve.

"We've got to get out on the other side," said Tuan.

But when they had dashed round the willow tree and the pagoda they pulled up short.

"The cheats!" cried Chris. "They've only *painted* the door this side."

In all the four outer walls there was only one real door that opened, to let the electricians bring in the lights. It was the one they had come in by. They crept cautiously back to it and peeped out.

Steve drew back quickly. "There she is!"

The white figure of Mrs Maltby was crawling into the shell of the dark dragon. In the road below a knot of motorists were arguing furiously and waving their arms. A young policeman stood looking from

18

one to the other. Then he made up his mind and came striding towards the traffic island. The angry drivers shouted after him. But he made straight for the dragon.

"Quick!" said Tuan. "Go behind those rocks."

He darted across the brightly lit grass into the deep shadows. Steve followed. Chris took a deep breath and started to run.

"CHRIS CHUDLEY! STOP!" thundered the dragon.

Chris froze in the full glare of the floodlights. He dared not move. Slowly he watched with horror as the policeman seized the rear of Mrs Maltby's raincoat and began to haul her backwards out of the

hole. The dragon gave a loud yelp of surprise. Chris covered his eyes.

"Now then!" The policeman demanded. "What are you up to in there?"

Chris didn't wait to hear any more. He began to run. The others were in front of him, racing down the slope towards the edge of the road. The cars that hadn't bumped into each other were starting to move. Tuan was already at the kerbside, waiting for a chance to cross.

Then to crown it all, in the glare of the second dragon, Steve skidded in the mud. He tumbled on to his face and began to roll, down towards the edge of the roundabout. Tuan ran to stop him, but he was not strong enough to hold Steve's weight alone. The two of them were slithering fast out into the path of the surging traffic. Chris launched himself into a flying rugby tackle. He hit the ground and pinned Steve's ankles beneath him. They slid a few more inches and stopped. Together he and Tuan hauled Steve upright.

"Can't you do anything right!" groaned Chris. "Now I've got mud all down my front as well. We haven't all got washing machines, you know."

"I like that!" Steve protested. "It wasn't me that exploded the dragon."

20

The cars that had been sweeping past were now honking furiously at the arguing drivers.

"Move!" ordered Chris. And they darted across the road to the pavement and round the safety of the corner.

"We did it!" cheered Steve. "We escaped the dragons *and* the sharks and the evil magicians."

"*You* may have," said Chris gloomily. "But she recognised me. You wait till tomorrow morning. There'll be enough flames and smoke coming out of her office for a hundred dragons. *And* we didn't find any treasure."

But as it happened, he didn't have to wait till morning. He had hardly finished tea when the doorbell rang.

"Chris Chudley?" asked the policeman. Not that he needed to.

It wasn't the young constable who had grabbed Mrs Maltby. This was a big, broad inspector with bushy eyebrows that he brought together in a fierce frown.

"Yes," admitted Chris. It wasn't the first time he and Inspector Brooks had met, by a long way.

"Mind if I come in?" The Inspector scratched his head, "This time you've given me a bit of a problem, young man. From what your headmistress has been

21

telling me, I don't know whether I ought to be putting you behind bars or giving you a medal. First you damage valuable Council property. Then you cause a moving traffic accident. And then you top it all off by saving your two friends from a very sticky end."

Chris blinked. He hadn't been expecting that. What had Mrs Maltby said?

"By rights, I should give you a stiff caution. Still, Christmas is coming, so I'll keep the sermon short. From what I hear, your Mrs Maltby is planning to do that bit a whole lot better than I can when she sees you in the morning. So I'll let you off with a solemn warning. Dragons are dangerous. You stay away from them in future."

"Some hopes of that," murmured Chris.

"*What* did you say?"

"I said, yes, I will! Sorry!"said Chris hastily.

But he knew he would not be able to stay away from dragons. Not with a headmistress like Mrs Maltby.

2

A Mouthful of Fire

It was the Hindu feast of Divali. Mr Downes let them decorate the classroom with paper flowers and light a row of candles on his desk.

"Put that one down, Chris," he ordered. "It's not a sparkler. If you burn the school down, I'll be out of a job."

"My Dad might be in one for a change," said Steve. "He's a brickie. Well, he was."

Shiwan showed them how to make pictures out of sand and little stones.

"At home, we do it with rice," she said.

Chris put bits of stick in his and made a gun. Tuan made a beautiful picture of a ship sailing into the sunset. Chris leaned over Lisa's shoulder.

"What's that meant to be? It looks like a broken teapot."

"It's a lotus flower, *of course*. Can't you see? Shiwan

23

says Lakshmi always sits on one."

"Looks as if it could be painful," said Chris. "Who's Lakshmi, when she's at home?"

"This is her festival. And don't step on her," Shiwan told him. "She's the goddess of wealth."

Chris moved his foot carefully off Shiwan's picture.

"No kidding? She could come in handy. I think I'll become a Hindu. I can't afford Christmas this year."

"Then you must put many lights in your window and leave the door open and invite Lakshmi into your house for the coming year."

"That's no good. I haven't got any money for candles. She's got it all wrong. She ought to go to the houses where it's dark. They're the ones who've had the electric cut off for fiddling the meter."

Shiwan had brought a tray of Indian food which she passed around at playtime. There were sweets made with coconut and sugar, and another plate with round golden balls. Chris took one and bit into it carefully.

"What's this? Mashed potato? It doesn't taste of much."

Shiwan caught Rahat's eye and they both giggled. They watched Chris chew slowly. Then the hot spices hit the back of his throat like an explosion.

"Cor!" He spat the rest of it on to the floor. "It's deep-fried dynamite!"

Shiwan and Rahat collapsed into fits of laughter.

"Chris," bellowed Mr Downes. "What do you think you're doing? Get out of the room, you little pig!"

"Well, it ought to have a government health warning," Chris protested. "Can't I have another of them coconut things to take the taste away?"

"No, you can't. If you behave like an animal, you can spend the rest of playtime in the yard."

Chris went outside. Tuan picked up another of the peppery balls and followed him. He grinned at Chris.

"They're good," he said. "Would you like half of this one?"

"Ugh! No thanks. I think I'll stick to Christmas, after all. I'd rather have mince pies."

"That was great, on the roundabout," said Tuan. "I didn't know you had dragons at Christmas."

"We don't usually," said Chris. "It's supposed to be shepherds and angels and baby Jesus."

"We used to have Chinese New Year. With a dancing dragon. He goes through the streets. Sometimes he looks in at windows and people give him money."

"Get away. Father Christmas gives *us* presents. At least, that's what it's like in the pictures. Sacks of presents and turkey and plum pudding. Only I reckon he's been a bit skint lately. Guess what we had for Christmas dinner last year? Sausage and chips and a Mars bar." He kicked the fence and laughed. "Yeah. Well, I *like* sausages. Might be better this year, though. My Mum's got a job, cleaning the pet shop down Bridge Street. She sweeps up parrot-droppings and all that stuff. Hey, that's a thought!

We could have stuffed parrot for Christmas dinner. That'd be different!"

"But no more dragons?"

"Yeah. Of course we've got one. Only they usually call her the headmistress."

And that was when Chris made his second mistake that morning.

"Do they indeed?" a voice grated behind them.

The two boys swung round. Mrs Maltby, the headmistress, was glaring down at them. Chris's mouth fell open.

"Crumbs!" he said softly.

"Exactly. What is *that* you've got scattered all down your jumper?"

"Fried gunpowder," muttered Chris, brushing the

crumbs away. "At least that's what it tasted like."

"I thought Mr Downes' class was having a party for Divali. Don't tell me he's had to throw you out of the room *again*, Chris Chudley."

"It wasn't my fault! It was that Shiwan. She should have warned us. You're supposed to fly red flags when you serve people live ammunition."

Mrs Maltby turned to Tuan.

"And when does *your* dragon dance?" she asked.

Tuan gave her a puzzled look. "Please?"

"This Chinese New Year. When is it?"

"I don't know how soon. But it is in the winter."

"Hm. We must find out. And as for *you!*" She fixed her steely eyes on Chris. "I warned Mr Downes that Chris Chudley and candles would be a dangerous mixture."

"It wasn't the candles. I hardly touched them. It was that dynamite dumpling."

"Then, if you've been eating dynamite, you had better move out of range before it explodes. I understand that dragons are in the habit of breathing fire."

Chris and Tuan moved away from the fence. Chris whistled softly.

"Just my luck she had to be listening. They say that elephants never forget. Do you think dragons do?"

28

3

Chris's Big Chance

Mr Downes was having a bad day.

Chris could tell that by the way he kept jumping up from his desk and shouting, "For the last time, work QUIETLY!"

That was the third time he had said, "For the last time . . ." But still nothing happened. It never did.

Every time Mr Downes said it, he sat down again at his desk, and disappeared. There was a crowd of children all round him, having their books marked, so he could not see what was happening at the back of the classroom.

Jimmy was tying Rahat's pigtail to the back of her chair. Very gently, so she would not notice until she stood up. Kim had stolen Angela's felt-tips and was sticking them through Lisa's black curls. Lisa looked like a multi-coloured hedgehog.

Chris looked round the classroom. He was bored.

On the other side of the room was the goldfish tank, standing on a bookcase. Chris wondered if he could fire his rubber right into the middle of the water. That would surprise the goldfish.

It was a difficult shot. The rubber would have to drop before it hit the window.

Chris held the rubber on the end of his ruler. He bent the ruler back.

PING! He watched the blue rubber sail across the room. Over Angela and Sally's heads. Over Tuan and Ben's heads. It was starting to drop now. But not soon enough.

It hit the flowers on the window-sill. The green vase rocked, and swayed, and toppled over.

SMASH! The broken vase rolled to the edge of the window-sill, right over the goldfish tank.

CRASH! SPLASH! It went tumbling into the tank.

A tidal wave rose out of the tank. Carried on its back was the struggling goldfish. The wave of water hit Rahat on the neck. She screamed and leaped to her feet. The chair, which Jimmy had tied to her pigtail, came with her. Rahat screamed louder and swung round. The chair swung too, and knocked little Tuan over.

Everyone else jumped up and started yelling. They crowded round Rahat. It took a long time to untie her pigtail. Rahat was hitting everyone she could reach. The only one who was not yelling was Tuan. He just lay on the floor and laughed.

In the middle of all this, the little goldfish made one last desperate flick with its tail and went sailing across the room to the floor. It lay slithering and gasping for breath, among all the stamping feet.

Chris jumped on to the table.

"Look out! It's a flying fish. Don't step on it!"

With a Tarzan cry, he jumped over Steve and down on to the floor. He made a flying tackle through the crowd of legs and caught the goldfish in his hands.

"It's all right, Sir! I've got it!" he yelled, waving it in the air.

"SIT DOWN!" bellowed Mr Downes for the fifth time.

The class straggled back to their seats, with everyone blaming everyone else in loud voices. Chris stood in the middle of the room with the dusty goldfish in his hands.

"I said, SIT DOWN," said Mr Downes.

"I can't, Sir. What shall I do with it?"

"Do with what?"

"The goldfish, Sir. It was on the floor. Under Rahat's chair."

"I never done it! I never touched the goldfish!" shouted Rahat.

"Shut up, Rahat." said Mr Downes. He beamed at Chris. "Good boy! I'm glad someone round here has a bit of sense, though I didn't think it would be you. Now, put it back in the tank."

Chris walked across the room and put the goldfish back in the green water. A film of dust and pencil-shavings floated to the surface. The goldfish dived under a stone and disappeared.

Chris smiled at the cloudy water. That had livened up the afternoon though it was a good job Mr Downes didn't know how the fish had got on the floor.

"Right. Now that the excitement is over, we'll get down to business again. But if I find out who started it, I'll have his guts for garters. Now gather round."

The rest of the class sat on the floor, on the chairs, on the tables, round Mr Downes. Chris sat on the electric heater.

"Get off the heater, Chris. We don't want the classroom to smell of roast pork."

"Are you calling me a pig?" said Chris indignantly.

"You said it, not me. Now get off."

Chris wriggled down very slowly from the warm heater. It was near Christmas. The heater was the best place to sit on a cold day.

"Pig yourself," he muttered. Then he looked to see if Mr Downes had heard him. He hadn't, which was just as well. You could go too far, even with Mr Downes.

"Now," said Mr Downes. "The Christmas play."

Half the class surged forward in excitement. Hands waved in the air.

"Please, Sir, can I be Mary?"

"Please, Sir, I want to be a king!"

"Sir, can we have a real lamb, like the other class did last year?"

"I could bring a donkey, Sir! At my sister's school they had a donkey!"

Chris nudged Steve. "If he makes me an angel, I'll throw up."

"SHUT UP!" roared Mr Downes. "Right. Now that it's about as quiet as a tonne of bricks falling off an eighteen-storey building on to corrugated iron, perhaps you'll listen to me. We'll have to see who can read the best, before we decide who gets which parts. First, Mary."

"Me!"

"Me!"

"Me!"

"Angela," said Sally, pushing her friend forward.

"Sally," said Angela, pushing Sally.

"Lisa," said Mr Downes. And then, "Good heavens, Lisa. What have you got in your hair?"

Lisa hastily pulled the felt-tips out of her curly hair.

"They're Kim's," she said.

"They're not. They're Angela's," said Kim.

Angela looked in her pencil-case. "You pinched

34

them," she cried. "You cow!"

"ANGELA . . . ! Right, Lisa. Read this."

Lisa took the sheet of paper and began to read.

Chris was looking at Tuan, sitting in front of him. There was a tiny hole in the back of Tuan's jumper. Just one broken stitch. Chris got out his pencil and pressed it very carefully through the hole. Tuan turned round. He did not say anything. He just looked at Chris and smiled. He must be the only boy in the class who never got told off for making a noise.

Mr Downes said Lisa was going to be Mary.

"We need Joseph next."

On the edge of the hole in Tuan's jumper, there was a tiny loose end of wool. Just a little grey wisp, about a millimetre long.

Chris frowned. Very carefully, his finger and thumb closed on the little wisp of wool. He kept very still, but Tuan did not turn round again. Very, very gently, Chris started to pull.

Steve read the part of Joseph.

The little end of wool was about half a centimetre long now.

Paul read the part of Joseph.

One centimetre, two centimetres. The hole was getting bigger.

Jimmy read the part of Joseph.

"Terrible," said Mr Downes.

The wool hung down Tuan's back now in crinkles and loops. It was long enough to wind into a little ball.

"Chris!" said Mr Downes sharply.

Chris jumped, and dropped his little ball of wool.

"Yes, Sir?" He didn't know what Mr Downes wanted.

"Come on, boy. We haven't got all day. We've got three kings, four shepherds and Herod's army to get through before tea-time."

Chris looked round, puzzled. Steve nudged him.

"Go on. He wants you to read it."

Chris picked his way forward over the legs and knees to the front of the classroom. He took the sheet of paper that Mr Downes was holding out to him.

"Read it, then," said Mr Downes. "Wake up!"

Chris read,

"The hills have made us weary; we need a place to rest.
Look, Mary, Bethlehem! Now God be blessed."

There was a lot more like that.

He got to the end of the page and stopped. He looked up. The room was quiet. Everyone was looking at him.

"Very *good!*" said Mr Downes in surprise. "I'd never have believed it, but I think you've got it."

"Got what?" said Chris.

"The part," said Mr Downes. "Don't you know what you've been reading? This may be the biggest mistake of my teaching career, but I've just made you Joseph."

Joseph. Him? He had to be joking. No one ever gave Chris Chudley parts like that.

But Mr Downes just had. Now he was busy with the Angel Gabriel.

Chris picked his way back to Steve and sat down.

The hole in Tuan's jumper was quite big. You could see his blue shirt showing through. Chris wished he hadn't done it now. Still, he couldn't knit the stitches back again.

He picked up the little ball of wool and started to push it inside the hole, out of sight. Tuan turned round and smiled.

"You're tickling."

"It's all right," said Chris. "You've got a hole in your jumper. I was just tidying it up."

He crossed his arms and held his hands very tightly against his sides so that they would not get into any more mischief. He would try very hard to be good now.

37

The reading went on. Kings. Shepherds. Herod. Everyone was getting bored and noisy. Mr Downes picked up his papers.

"Right. That's it. The rest of you horrible lot will be a chorus of angels. No! Hang on! There's one more I've forgotten. We need an inn-keeper. It's a very small part. He just has to open the door when Joseph and Mary come looking for a bed. Then he shakes his head and says, '*No, every room is full. Be off. You heard what I said.*'"

He looked round hopefully. But nearly everyone had a part now. Some of the girls waved their hands in the air, and so did Steve. But Chris waved his harder.

"Sir!" he shouted. "What about Tuan? He could do it."

Steve scowled at him. "What about *me?*"

Mr Downes looked thoughtful. "All right then, Tuan. Come and try it."

Tuan stood at the front and read the words in his small, clear voice. You could only just hear him at the back of the room.

"That was a rotten idea," muttered Chris. "He makes as much noise as a mouse that's had its tonsils out."

"Hm," said Mr Downes doubtfully. "You'll have

38

to shout a lot louder. But at least the words were clear. Right. You're the inn-keeper. That's everyone now."

"It must be my lucky day for once," said Chris, as they walked out of school. "Me, Joseph! Cor, my Mum's not going to believe this."

"It's all right for some," said Steve. "Now I'm a flipping angel."

4

Trouble on Stage

Next day they had the first rehearsal. Mr Downes came in with an armful of papers, like Mum with a pile of sheets on wash day. He gave out a part to everyone.

Chris looked at his. "*Joseph*", it said on the first page. He turned over. "*Joseph*", it said again. He turned on a few more pages. "*Joseph*", "*Joseph*", "*Joseph*". There seemed to be no end to it.

He nudged Steve. "Look at this. I'll never learn this lot by Christmas. I bet even James Bond doesn't have this much to learn. How big's your part."

"Three pages," said Steve. "We've got to *sing* half of it!"

"Flipping cheek," said Chris. "Look at all mine. I ought to get double time at least, for this."

"You are," said Steve. "I'm getting nothing, and so are you. Twice nothing is nothing. Satisfied?"

"No," said Chris. "I'm going to start a union."

But nobody was expected to learn the words the first day. They read their parts and walked up and down a bit, without bothering about the actions.

Chris read his part in a loud, clear voice. Mr Downes seemed quite pleased with him.

Joseph and Mary got to the inn at Bethlehem. They asked for a room. Tuan shook his head, and said his one line, and closed the door in their faces. But Kim, who was the inn-keeper's wife, slipped out and showed them the way to the stable. Then all the exciting things started to happen.

The baby was born. Sally was going to bring her doll for that. At least, that was what Sally said. But Angela said her doll was nicer than Sally's, and she wanted to bring hers. And Sally said that was silly, because Angela's doll had fair hair and blue eyes, and Jesus wouldn't have fair hair and blue eyes. And Angela said he wouldn't have black curly hair and brown skin, like Sally's doll, either. And Sally said, how do you know, he might have. And Angela said, he didn't, so there.

In the end, Mr Downes said that Lisa had black curly hair, and she was playing Mary, so Sally's doll sounded just right. And Sally made a rude face at Angela, to show she had won. And Angela hit Sally.

41

When Mr Downes had sorted them out, and the rest of the class had stopped cheering for one or the other, they went back to the play, with Angela and Sally looking like two very cross angels.

The angels sang a song. At least, they would be singing it later, but Mr Downes didn't have the music, so they just said it. And Mary thanked them.

The angels came to the shepherds. And the shepherds came to the stable and gave presents. And Mary thanked them.

Chris turned over the page. There was nothing about Joseph here.

The wise men came following the star. They went to King Herod. They came to Bethlehem.

Chris turned over several more pages. Still nothing about Joseph. He just stood there at the back, behind Mary and the manger. People came into the stable, and knelt down and offered gifts, and went away. But nobody bothered about Joseph.

All sorts of things happened outside. But Joseph just went on standing there behind Mary and the manger.

Being Joseph was beginning to get boring. Chris felt in his pockets. He thought he might have a bit of chewing gum left. He remembered having to stick some in his pocket in a hurry last week, when Mrs Maltby had looked straight at him in prayers. That had been a close thing. Mrs Maltby had the sort of grey eyes that went through you like double-edged razor blades. If he'd been one second later, she would have stopped the hymn right in the middle of a verse, and her voice would have come slicing through the hall towards him.

"Boy! Are you *chewing?*"

And everyone would have been turning round and trembling at the knees. He had got rid of the chewing gum just in time.

But it wasn't in his pocket now. Mum must have shifted it. She had a habit of turning his pockets out at the weekend. You had to be careful what you left in them.

There was something else instead. His hand closed round a small, hard tin. He drew it out behind Lisa's back and looked at it.

"AIR RIFLE PELLETS", it said in red letters on blue. It wasn't, though. He and Steve were going fishing after school, along the canal.

Chris opened the lid a little. The maggots were all there. Fat, creamy-white, alive. Gently stirring and squirming.

He closed the lid again. The kings were in the stable now. They were kneeling down. Making long speeches about gold, and frankincense, and myrrh. Chris looked at his part again. It went on and on. He didn't have anything to say till the page before the end. He just had to stand here, behind Lisa, listening to everyone else.

It was all right for Lisa. She was sitting down, being Mary. Showing off. She still had plenty to say. He looked down at all the black curls of her head. She had looked funny yesterday, with Angela's felt-tip pens stuck through them, like a porcupine.

Today, they were just plain black curls, like wire springs. There was a hole in the middle of each one. It would look much more interesting if there were something in the middle of each curl. Something quite small, so that Mr Downes wouldn't notice.

Very gently, Chris opened the tin of maggots. When he picked one up it felt soft and squishy. If he squeezed it too hard it would burst, like a split sausage. He placed it very carefully in the middle of one of Lisa's curls. It lay there, squirming very slightly. White against black. He tried another.

Lisa fidgeted a little. Chris would have to be careful. It would be a pity to spoil it when it was beginning to look interesting.

He laid a row of white maggots across the back of Lisa's head. Then a column going up to the top. Then another two rows. Some of the maggots just lay there, curled up in the nests of hair. Some of them stirred sleepily.

The kings went away. Lisa bent over the manger. Chris couldn't reach her head now, but he could see the lines of white dots in her hair. He was pleased with them. The angels came back and gathered round the manger.

Suddenly Angela yelled, "Worms! She's got worms in her hair!"

Everyone stopped and stared. Then they all started shouting. Lisa clapped her hands to her head and came away with a maggot between her fingers. She took one look at it, screamed, and was sick all over the floor.

For a few minutes there was so much fuss that nobody bothered about Chris. He dodged round to the other side of the room and hid behind the shepherds. But it couldn't last. As soon as the girls had finished screaming over the maggots, and the boys had stopped making sick noises about the mess on the floor, and Tuan had picked all the maggots out of Lisa's hair and dropped them in the waste-paper basket, Mr Downes turned round on Chris.

"And as . . . as . . . for . . . YOU! You will go to the caretaker, and get a bucket and a mop, and clean up this mess."

"I'm not mopping up after her!" said Chris indignantly. "How do I know what she's had for dinner?"

"It's either that—or you go straight to Mrs

46

Maltby. And that's your *Very . . . Last . . . Warning!*"

He was doing a fair imitation of Mrs Maltby himself. Using that nasty, grating voice, not shouting like he usually did. Chris knew the signals. He had gone too far. He went and got the bucket.

But at the end of school, he collected all the maggots out of the waste-paper basket and put them back in the tin. It was a pity to waste good money.

5

Too Many Words

"I thought I told you to clear the table," Chris's mum said. "What are you doing? It's worse than what you have to fill in for the Social, all those bits of paper."

Chris shut his eyes tight.

"*I have cut a stout stick. Mary, you shall ride.*

I have cut a stout stick . . ."

No, he'd said that bit twice. He opened his eyes and looked at the paper again. His mother smacked his hand away.

"There, now you've got tomato sauce all over it. That Mr Heinz must have made his fortune out of what you leave on your plate."

Chris put his hands over his ears.

"*I am a donkey. Mary, you shall ride . . .*"

No. That *couldn't* be right, could it?

"Sounds like poetry. I thought you didn't get

homework till you got to the big school."

"It isn't homework. It's our play."

"What play's that, then?"

"For Christmas. You know. Angels. Shepherds, Donkey."

"You never said you were in a play."

"I just have. He only told us yesterday."

"I was in a school play once. It was all about the weather forecast. I was Little Depression over the Atlantic. Boring, that was. I'd rather have been Hurricane. What are you, then?"

"Joseph." He watched her face.

"*Joseph?* In a Nativity play? Get away. You're having me on. But what about all them other kids? What did they choose you for?"

"Why shouldn't they?"

"Fancy that. Our Chris, Joseph. You just wait till I tell your gran. She'll be tickled pink. Here, I tell you what! If her chest's better, I'll bring her to see it, shall I? When is it?"

"The week before Christmas."

Chris's heart fell as he said it. Three weeks. He would never learn all these words in time. It wasn't possible. And now Mum was going to go and bring Gran as well. Mum had never come to school before. Not in all the years he'd been going. But then, Chris had never been allowed to do anything worth seeing.

But she was coming to this. The hall would be full of people. All the other mums would be there. And the teachers. And Mrs Maltby in the front row with all the nobs in posh clothes. And they would all have come to watch him being Joseph, and Lisa being Mary. He'd *never* learn his part in time.

But he felt better next week when Mr Downes and Miss Jones brought in all the costumes for them to try on. Chris could see the gown he wanted. It was a red and yellow striped one, with a white head-dress.

The three kings were fighting over their crowns. Lisa put her white veil over her face and did a voodoo dance to frighten everyone, till Mr Downes told her not to be silly. He picked up the red and yellow costume.

"Here you are, Chris. I think this one is yours."

Chris couldn't believe his luck. Everything was going right for him.

The gown fitted. He held up his arms in the big, loose sleeves. Then he wrapped it round him and walked up and down the stage. He felt very grand. Just think. Him, playing the leading part. If he hadn't read so well, he might have had to be an *angel*, like

Steve, or the inn-keeper, like Tuan, with only one line to say.

"I want all you shepherds to wear sandals. You, too, Joseph," said Mr Downes.

Chris's heart sank.

"Please, Sir. I haven't got any sandals."

"He can borrow mine," said Steve quickly.

The angels had bare, cold feet.

"Right. Take your costumes off and fold them up neatly. Angela, you idiot! I didn't mean crease your wings in half. Give me patience! Now, put your scripts away. You should all have learned your words by now. Chris and Lisa. It's you to start."

Everyone scuttled away to the sides of the room. The stage was empty except for Chris and Lisa. Everyone was waiting for Joseph.

Waiting . . . and waiting. You could hear the electric clock on the wall whirring. But no words would come.

"Chris?" said Mr Downes, looking worried.

But Chris's mind was as empty as the school hall. He did not know the words. Without his sheets of paper, he was lost.

In the silence, someone whispered behind him.

"*Good news, Mary . . .*"

Through a crack in the curtains, Chris caught a

glimpse of little Tuan's smiling face, mouthing the words.

Chris was so glad, he shouted them out loud and clear.

"*Good news, Mary, the best news of my life.*

Your father has promised me that you shall be my wife."

He had got it right. But on the next page he dried up again. Mr Downes slammed down his script.

"Chris! Have you *learned* this part?"

"Yes, Sir! It's just that my mind keeps going blank."

"It'll go permanently blank if you mess up this rehearsal once more. If you can't be bothered to learn the words, just say so. There's plenty of other people who could take your part."

"I have learned it, Sir! Honest, Sir."

"Then get on with it,"

Once again, Tuan's comforting whisper stole through the curtains. Chris seized on it, and the play went on. Mr Downes stopped looking worried. But Chris knew that it would happen again in the next scene, and the next. He didn't know his part yet.

He went off the stage, feeling rather sick. He wished he had not got himself into this. But he did want to be Joseph. He would never get another chance like this. He *would* learn the words. He'd have to. But he needed more time.

Someone plucked at his sleeve. It was Tuan again. Waiting behind the curtains to be the inn-keeper. To shake his head, and say his one line, and shut the door.

"Chris. Put your costume on again. You can hide your words up your sleeve. Then Mr Downes won't see."

Chris looked down at Tuan. It was brilliant. So simple.

"Thanks, Tuan. It must be nice to be a genius."

Tuan smiled back at him happily and held up the red and yellow gown.

As Chris stepped back on to the stage Mr Downes bellowed at him.

"What on earth are you playing at now? It's not the dress rehearsal."

"I know, Sir. But I thought it might help me remember. Make me feel more *like* Joseph."

"Well . . . OK, then. But I warn you. If you muck up that costume, you'll be out. Finished."

"I won't, Sir. I'll be ever so good."

He was extra careful to behave himself, even in the boring bits. And it worked. If Chris kept his arms folded, and squinted down past his left elbow, he could just about read the words. Enough to keep him going, anyway, though it was tricky turning over the pages without Mr Downes noticing.

And all the time, there was Tuan's small face peeping through the back curtains and whispering Chris's part to himself, word-perfect.

6

Almost the Last Straw

It was raining down by the canal. A steady, cold
rain, making bubbles on the surface of the water.
Down the path were two big, green umbrellas,
sheltering fishermen. Chris and Steve did not have
an umbrella. They had pulled their hoods round their
faces. The rain dripped off their noses. They had
been holding their fishing-rods for two hours now
in icy hands, but the fish were not biting.

Steve had a pile of paper on his knee. At first, the
paper had been white. Now his wet jeans were
staining it an inky blue. If he turned the sodden
pages any more, the paper would fall to pieces.

Steve said, "Then Tuan opens the door and *you*
say . . ."

Chris stared into the nearest bubble and chanted,

"*Have you any room for us? My wife must have a
bed.*"

"That's it, Chris! You've got it! Then Tuan sends you away, and Kim comes out and shows you to the stable, and that's you finished till the last page."

"Learning it's one thing. Remembering it's another. My mum's coming. She's bringing Gran. I'll forget my words. I know I will."

"You won't. Anyway, Tuan knows them. He knows everyone's words. He'll help you out."

"It's funny, that. When he came here, he couldn't speak a word of English. Now he's better than anyone. And he's only got one line to say. It's not fair, is it?"

Steve stood up. The wet paper was coming to pieces in his hand.

"Do you want this any more?"

57

Chris looked at it for the last time.

"No, You're right. If I don't know it now, I never will. I hope Mr Downes is grateful, that's all. I've never worked so hard for that flipping school in my whole life. Learning all that."

Steve threw a handful of soggy paper into the canal. A fish jumped straight out of the water and snapped at it.

"Blooming cheek," said Chris. "That's the first one we've seen all afternoon. I'm going to use that paper for ground bait next time. It's cheaper than bread."

It was the day before the dress rehearsal.

Mr Downes was ticking off the things they needed on his fingers.

"Costumes, shepherds' crooks. An apology for a donkey . . ."

"I could have brought a real one. At my sister's school play they had a real one," said Kim.

"Shut up. Paul's horse on wheels will have to do, with a pair of false ears. The door of the inn. Sally's doll. The manger . . . Pity we haven't got some real hay for that."

Chris's hand shot up.

"Sir! Sir! I can get some hay. My Mum cleans for Mr Spiers. You know. Mr Spiers at the pet shop. I can get things cheap there. He'd let us have some hay, Sir. Shall I ask him?"

"It's a bit late. I wish you'd said sooner. We want it today."

"We can go now, Sir. Steve will come with me. Can we, Sir?"

Mr Downes looked doubtful. "I'd take you round in my car. Only I daren't leave this lot on their own. Oh, OK. Here's some money. And I want the change. No nonsense, mind. Straight there. Straight back, and no messing. Can I trust you for once?"

"Of course you can, Sir. You know us."

"That's what I mean," said Mr Downes grimly.

He let them go. Chris and Steve walked along the cold, sunny pavement to the shops in Bridge Street. Mr Spiers' pet shop smelt of dog biscuits and parrots. He also kept a Great Dane called Fred, that filled up half the shop and slobbered over customers.

"It eats shop-lifters," whispered Chris. "It's been trained."

Mr Spiers was in the back of the shop. When he heard what they wanted, he dragged out a bale of hay and waved away the money Chris held out.

"Christmas comes but once a year," he said, "Have this one on me."

There was a fat man in the shop, blowing smoke

rings at a mynah bird. The mynah bird huddled in a corner of its cage and coughed.

"Fred," said Mr Spiers quietly.

The Great Dane stood up and put two huge paws on the fat man's shoulders. The fat man turned round, jumped two feet in the air and dropped his cigarette.

"Down, Fred," said Mr Spiers. "Can I help you, sir?"

Chris bent down very fast and scooped up the half-smoked cigarette. He put it in his pocket. Then he picked up the string on one side of the hay bale, and Steve took the other side. They set off back to school.

The bale of hay was heavy. But it was a nice, sunny morning. They put the hay down on the pavement halfway along the street and lay down with their heads against it for a rest. People looked at the boys a bit oddly as they stepped over them, but

Chris and Steve didn't mind.

At the next corner they rested again, and changed hands. And then halfway along the last street. And then at the school gate.

"All change," said Chris for the last time.

The playground was deserted. Halfway across, Chris took a sharp turn to the right. Steve fell over his feet and the string came off the bale and there was hay all over the playground.

"Can't you do anything right?" said Chris.

"I didn't know where you were going."

"Time for a quick drag," said Chris. "No one will miss us."

They went into the boys' toilets, leaving a trail of hay behind them. Steve watched while Chris got out the half-smoked cigarette and a box of matches.

"You don't really smoke, do you? I never seen you."

"Don't often get the chance, do I?"

He lit the cigarette and began to puff at it. His face screwed up in an odd expression.

"Do you *like* doing that?" asked Steve curiously.

"I dunno," said Chris, coughing.

"Then why do you do it?"

"That's not the point, is it? Liking it."

"There's a funny smell," said Steve.

"There always is in these toilets."

"No. Not that. More like . . . burning. Chris!"

A wisp of dark smoke floated past Chris's ear. He jumped up from the bale and whirled round.

"The hay!" shouted Steve. "You've gone and set fire to it!"

The tiny blue flames were almost too small to see. But they darted across the surface of the bale like live things, and everywhere they went the charred and smouldering patch grew bigger and bigger. Chris beat at it wildly with his hands.

Steve was jumping up and down with excitement. "Can I smash the fire alarm? I've been dying to do that for years. Go on, can I Chris?"

"I'll smash your head in, if you do," Chris growled. "Here, if you want to do something useful, jump up and down on this for a change."

They tore the bale apart and stamped on the hay until it was a dead and blackened mess. Chris scooped up as much of the ashes as he could, dumped them in the lavatory pan and pulled the chain. When it had finished, bits of charred hay still floated sadly on the water. The floor was black. They threw water over it and swilled it about with their shoes, but it only seemed to spread the soot further. Even Chris looked shaken.

He pushed the rest of the hay back into a bundle and tied it up again. It drooped untidily and the string hung slackly round it.

"It doesn't look too good, does it?" said Steve. What's Mr Downes going to say?"

"He can't *prove* anything."

Chris pulled the chain again, and the last of the blackened stems disappeared. They lugged the bale back to the classroom, dropping even more of it as they went.

Mr Downes looked at it suspiciously.

"Is that a bale of hay or a pig's nest?"

"Yeah, well, it's not a standard size. But Mr Spiers let us have it cheap."

"Free," corrected Steve.

Chris kicked him. "Oh, yeah. Free. Here's your money back, Sir."

"Just a minute. Let's have a look at your hands!"

He turned over Chris's sooty palms.

"Go on. Tell me. What have you been up to this time?"

"Me, Sir? Nothing, Sir."

"Then you won't mind turning out your pockets, will you?"

Steve produced a dirty hanky and his dinner-money. Chris's heart sank. He reached into

63

his own trousers. One by one the bits and pieces fell on to Mr Downes' desk. A piece of old chewing gum with a dead cockroach embedded in it, Kim's rubber with her name on it, a horror picture from a video magazine.

"Now the other one."

Slowly Chris took out the box of matches.

"I *see*," said Mr Downes heavily. "And the cigarettes?"

"Cigarettes, Sir? Get off. Where would I get ciggies? You can search me if you don't believe me."

Mr Downes wrinkled his nose in disgust and reached his hands into Chris's pockets. He came out with a fistful of mildewed crumbs.

"If I thought you'd been smoking . . ."

"*Me*, Sir?"

"Look, all you had to do was to walk down Bridge Street and back again. How did you get into that state?"

"There was this demolition site, see. They were having a bonfire. And me and Steve sat down for a rest."

"Is this true?"

Steve raised his round blue eyes to Mr Downes' face.

"There *was* a fire, sir."

Mr Downes stared hard at them both.

"Well, if you won't tell me, perhaps you'd like to explain to Mrs Maltby."

"No, Sir! Not Mrs Maltby," cried Chris, horrified. "*Please*, Sir!"

"Give me one good reason why not."

"We didn't do any damage. But she's not going to believe that. You know she's got it in for me, Sir." Then inspiration dawned. "She'd stop me being in the play, Sir. And it's the dress rehearsal tomorrow. You couldn't get anyone else to do it. She could spoil the whole thing. And all the parents are coming. And everybody's worked so hard. And Miss Jones has made the costumes . . ."

He watched the doubts struggling in Mr Downes' face.

"And I've learned all my lines. I've tried ever so hard, haven't I, Sir?"

There was an awful moment when he thought it wasn't going to work. But Mr Downes couldn't keep a straight face. He burst out laughing.

"OK, Chris! You win! I could forget to mention it till *after* the play. But I'm warning you, if you do just one more thing . . ."

"I'll be ever so good! I'll . . . I'll be an angel, Sir!"

"That'll be the day!"

Chris turned away, weak with relief. It had been a very close thing.

"Oh and Chris."

"Yes, Sir?"

"Every day from now on you'll turn out your pockets for me. And if ever I catch you with a box of matches again . . ."

"You won't, Sir, I promise, Sir. Never!"

7

The Curtain Falls

When the dress rehearsal started, Chris was so nervous he felt sick. But to his amazement he remembered every word of his lines. Not once did Tuan have to whisper to him through the curtains. By the time they got to the stable and he had finished his speaking part, he felt so exhausted he thought his legs would give way.

But after that, there was still the dull bit, when the bloke who wrote the play seemed to have forgotten he'd put Joseph in it. That was the trouble with this part. There was either too much of it or not enough.

It wasn't fair. Mary could sit down. Chris didn't see why he shouldn't, too. He sat down on the stage behind the manger.

"What are you doing, Chris? Get up."

"My legs are tired."

"Lean on your stick, then,"

"What stick?"

"The one it says in the script you're supposed to have cut."

"Well, I haven't."

"Then *get* one. By tomorrow. But you can't sit down."

"Lisa's sitting down."

"Lisa is Mary. You haven't had a baby."

"What about equal rights, then?"

"Look, do you want to be in this play, or don't you?"

"Yes, Sir!"

"Then stop messing about. There'll be a hall full of people watching you tomorrow."

After that, Chris thought he had better keep quiet. He didn't want to push his luck too far.

But his legs still ached. He stood on his right leg, to give the left one a rest. Then he stood on his left leg and rested the right one. Then he tried resting both of them at once, but that didn't work because he nearly fell over, and grabbed the manger, and *did* fall over, and he and Lisa ended up on the floor.

"CHRIS!"

"Sorry, Sir. I lost my balance."

"You'll lose your block, if it happens again."

Chris stood up again and watched the wise men

68

talking to Herod. He looked round. There was a curtain just behind him. It went all the way across the back of the stage. Grey velvet. It hung from big brass rings. The rings were round a wooden pole. And the pole was fastened to the brick wall at the back of the stage.

Chris took a handful of curtain and rested his weight on it. Let his arm hold him up for a change.

The kings had got to the stable at last. They were kneeling down offering their gifts. Chris's right arm grew tired. He shifted his weight to the other side and pulled on the curtain with his left hand.

There was a little rattle, and a shower of white dust fell on to the stage at his feet. Chris looked up. It came from the wall above him. One of the fastenings that held the pole to the bricks was coming away.

Still holding the curtain tightly, he moved round to look the other way. There was a louder rattle. Bits of red brick were falling on to the stage. The pole was beginning to tilt. The whole curtain was coming away from the wall. He watched the brass rings sliding down the pole. He caught a glimpse of great red holes appearing in the white wall. He saw the whole mass of grey curtain rushing towards him. He threw up his hands to save himself.

69

The pole hit him on the head. It knocked him forward on top of Lisa. And Lisa fell on top of the kings. And the kings toppled backwards into the angels. A great tidal wave of grey velvet came pouring down on top of everyone, cutting off the last muffled screams. Then there was silence, except for bits of brick thumping on to the stage.

After a while, Chris could hear other people scuffling about in the darkness, trying to get out. Lisa pushed him off, and went humping away under the curtain, like a caterpillar. Chris lay very still. Perhaps if Mr Downes thought the pole had knocked him out, things might be better.

Mr Downes dragged the curtain off him. Chris kept his eyes shut.

"Chris?"

He was right. Mr Downes sounded more anxious than cross.

"Mr *Downes!*"

Even with his eyes shut, Chris knew Mrs Maltby's voice. And he knew it was no use pretending with her. He opened his eyes quickly and scrambled to his feet.

The headmistress glared round at the wreckage. The dusty curtains all over the floor. The red holes in the wall where they had hung. The footprints on

the angels' white robes where they had climbed over each other. Her steely eyes came back to Chris. She advanced towards him. Chris backed away.

"I thought so! What has been going on here? And who is responsible for this?"

"It was an accident, Miss!"

"Yes, just an accident, Mrs Maltby," said Mr Downes hastily. "The pole fell down and hit one of the children. No bones broken. I'll see the caretaker. We'll have it fixed up again by tomorrow."

"Poles do not just *fall* down, Mr Downes. One of these children was to blame. Which of them was standing under it?"

"Chris Chudley. He was playing Joseph."

Mrs Maltby choked.

"You've . . . let . . . Chris Chudley . . . play . . . Joseph?"

"Yes, Mrs Maltby. He's got a lovely voice."

Mrs Maltby gave him a long, cold stare.

"Mr Downes. Let me make myself clear. I have invited two hundred parents to watch this play, and the school governors, and the vicar. Nothing must go wrong. Chris Chudley is *not* to play Joseph."

"But, Mrs Maltby . . ."

"I am not going to argue. There will no more *accidents*."

"But the play's tomorrow. It's too late to change parts. Chris is the only one who knows the words."

Chris held his breath. She'd have to let him do it, wouldn't she? After all the work he'd done.

And then Lisa dropped him in it. She'd never forgiven him for the maggots.

"Tuan knows all Joseph's words," she said sweetly. "Tuan knows the whole play by heart. Don't you, Tuan?"

Tuan looked unhappily from Lisa to Chris. He was not smiling this time. But Chris shrugged his shoulders and turned away. It was too late now. And it was true.

"Yes," said Tuan, in his small, clear voice.

"There you are, Mr Downes."

"OK. We'd better try it from the beginning," said Mr Downes wearily.

Miss Jones stood at the back of the hall and said she could *just* hear Tuan, but he'd have to shout a lot louder when the hall was full of people.

"Right, that settles it," said Mr Downes. "Tuan, you're Joseph. And Chris, you'll have to be the inn-keeper. One line, mind. Just one line. And if you get a single word wrong, so help me, I'll . . ."

"Yeah? You'll what?" said Chris, as Mr Downes turned away.

73

Mr Downes didn't hear. Even if he had, it couldn't be any worse than it was now. He'd lost the part. After all that learning.

"You wait," he muttered after the departing teachers. "Just you wait!"

8

The Surprise

"Will my green coat be all right? I'd wear my best, only it's lost two buttons. They won't all be dressed up posh, will they?"

"Only in the front row. Steve's Mum'll come in her jeans. I've never seen her in anything else."

"I wish I'd had my hair done."

"What's wrong with it? It looks the same as always."

"I know. Go on, cheer me up more. Still, it's not me they're going to be looking at, is it?"

He had tried to tell her. But the words wouldn't come. Chris's Mum hadn't been to school since the day he started. Other mums—dads, even—came to school for the Christmas play and the parents' evening and the summer fair. But not Chris's mum. She kept well away. He couldn't really blame her. Not with the sort of things Mr Downes threatened to say to her about Chris, if he ever saw her.

Chris felt sick. She was coming to school today for the first time. To see Chris. To watch him being Joseph in the Christmas play. For once in his life she thought he'd done something really good. She'd told the whole street. She was bringing Gran.

He couldn't tell her. He didn't know how to tell her that he'd made a mess of it. That he wasn't going to be Joseph any more. Just the inn-keeper. One line to say. One stupid line. He had to shake his head, and tell them there was no room at the inn, and shut the door. And that was him finished. The rest of the play would go on without him. She was wasting her time, coming to see him just do that.

"You don't *have* to come. It's not important."

"Of course we're coming."

He crawled away to school. He looked into the hall and scowled at the rows of empty seats. The inn-keeper's part wasn't worth bothering with. You could learn a part like that in five seconds. He'd rather not be in the play at all now. He even wondered about running away.

But he was still there when they started dressing up for the play. At least he still had his Joseph costume, with the red and gold stripes. He had tried Tuan's costume, but it only came down to his knees.

And the red and gold Joseph gown fell over Tuan like a collapsed parachute. So Mr Downes had said they had better keep their own.

They were all ready. The curtains at the front of the stage were shut. Chris was waiting at the back, hidden behind the inn door. He could hear the chatter from the hall.

Then he saw Mr Downes give the signal. The curtains opened. Tuan was standing in the middle of the stage, where Chris should have been. And all the mums went, "Aah!"

Somewhere out there in the hall, Chris's mum would be sitting with Gran. Looking at Joseph. Seeing it wasn't Chris. Wondering what had gone wrong. She'd told all her friends he was going to be Joseph.

He peeped through the crack in the inn door, and backed away. The school hall was full of people. Rows and rows of mums and dads and little brothers and sisters. And in the front row, Mrs Maltby, smiling at the vicar, and a lot of men in smart grey suits and ladies in posh coats and Sunday hats.

That Mrs Maltby. He'd get her some day. It was all her fault.

Joseph and Mary and the donkey were getting nearer. Any moment now, they'd be knocking at the

77

door. Any moment now, he'd have to say his one silly line.

"*No, every room is full. Be off. You heard what I said.*"

And that would be it. Finished. The play would go on without him, and all the interesting things would start to happen. That was what the other mums were waiting for.

Lisa would pick Sally's doll out of the manger, and Lisa's mum would go, "Aah!"

The angels would come trooping on in their white robes, and the angels' mums would go, "Aah!"

78

The shepherds would come with their lambs, and the shepherds' mums would go, "Aah!"

The kings would come in their bright robes and crowns, and the kings' mums would go, "Aah!"

But all Chris's mum would see was Chris shaking his head and shutting the door. Nobody would go "Aah!" about that.

Tuan knocked at the inn door. Chris heard it, but he didn't think anyone else would. So he knocked noisily himself, from the inside. Then he opened the door and stood there for everyone to see. Nobody said anything this time. They just waited.

Little Tuan smiled up at him and asked, *"Please have you any room for us? My wife must have a bed."*

And he stood there, smiling and waiting.

Everyone was waiting now. Waiting for Chris. Waiting for him to say there was no room at the inn. Waiting for the play to go on. And Chris began to smile too. Maybe it didn't have to be such a silly part, after all.

He looked down at the hall. They were all waiting. Mrs Maltby and the governors in their posh suits. The ladies in silly hats. The vicar. The mums and dads and grans, and little brothers and sisters. The teachers in the back row.

All waiting for Chris. Waiting for him to shake his head and shut the door. Waiting for all the best bits to start. For the stable, and the angels, and the shepherds, and the kings.

Tuan had stopped smiling now. He began to whisper the inn-keeper's words to Chris.

Chris smiled down at him kindly. He hadn't forgotten his line. But he wasn't going to say it now. An idea was growing in his mind. It was a lovely idea.

He smiled at Mrs Maltby and all the people in the hall. Just a little smile at first. But the smile got wider and wider. He smiled at Tuan's yellow face and Lisa's black one, till he was beaming a huge, happy, glorious welcome to them.

Then, with a flourish, he threw the inn door open

as wide as it would go. He pointed inside and said in a ringing voice,

"Room? Of course we've got room. *Hundreds* of rooms! It's Christmas, isn't it? Come in and make yourselves welcome, mate!"

There was a deathly silence.

And then the vicar began to laugh. And the men in Sunday suits began to laugh, and the ladies in hats, and the mums and dads and little brothers and sisters. The teachers in the back row were creasing themselves with laughter. And they were all standing up and clapping and cheering fit to bring the roof down, as Chris swept Tuan and Lisa into the inn and shut the door behind them.

The Dragon's Breath

After that it was the Christmas holidays, which was just as well, because it gave Mrs Maltby time to cool off a bit.

Now Tuan was painting another picture. This time it was a dragon. The dragon was gold and blue and red. It had a long red tongue and huge eyes. It had hundreds of feet. All around it, people were running through the street, letting off fireworks.

"Pow! Bang!" said Tuan happily.

Mr Downes leaned over and looked at the dragon picture.

"Of course!" he cried. "Chinese New Year!"

He turned to the rest of the class.

"How would you like to make a dragon for Tuan's New Year?"

"You're a bit late, aren't you?" said Chris. "It's nearly February."

"Years don't have to start on the first of January," said Mr Downes. "My birthday's in June. I'll be starting my twenty-fifth year . . . if I survive till then."

He told them about the dragon. The hundreds of feet were people underneath, dancing through the streets. The whole class cheered.

"It's better than a pantomime horse," said Steve. "A hundred times better."

"And when you make your dragon," said Mr Downes. "you paint its eye last of all. Because when you put in that last spot of paint, *the dragon comes to life*."

"Grr-OWW!" roared Chris.

And Angela screamed and fell off her chair.

Mr Downes fixed Chris with a cold stare.

"The dragon eats bad boys for breakfast. Chopped up, with bamboo shoots."

But Chris didn't believe him.

"What about fireworks?" said Chris. "Look, they're all letting them off like anything."

He pointed to Tuan's picture.

"Pow! Bang!" he said, nudging Tuan.

"Yes. We must have fireworks," said Tuan.

"No fireworks," said Mr Downes firmly. "Not with you lot. Absolutely not."

The class groaned. Tuan lost his smile. Chris leaned over the dragon-painting. He drew a body disappearing into the dragon's mouth, dripping blood. He drew an arrow pointing to it, and a label that said MR DOWNES. Then he drew another arrow pointing to the dragon's stomach. This time the label said MRS MALTBY.

They made a gorgeous dragon. They begged old curtains and sewed them together—red ones and gold ones and green ones, in slippery, shiny stuff. Then they cut dragon-scales out of Christmas wrapping paper, thousands and thousands of them, and stuck and sewed them on to the dragon's body. There was a long, swishing tail made out of old pyjama cord, with a huge gold tassel on the end.

And then there was the head. It started with egg-cartons, knobbly, like warts. Then they smoothed wet newspaper over it to build up the shape. Last of all, they painted it, gold and blue and scarlet. It had a huge red tongue, hanging from its jaws. The eyes were red too. But they were flat and lifeless. It was not time to paint in the last spot yet.

"Bags I be the head!" cried Chris, when they had put it together.

"No, me!"

"Me!"

Everyone wanted to be the dragon's head. Except Steve. He had tucked himself under the very end and was twirling the dragon's tail.

"Not you, Chris," said Mr Downes, pulling him away. "I want somebody sensible. Rahat's the best dancer. Good man, Steve. Yes, you can be the tail. Right, are you ready? Get in under and off we go!"

They didn't get far. It was dark under the curtains. After two steps they all fell over each other's feet.

"We'd better practise without the dragon, till we get the hang of it," said Mr Downes. "We've lost about three million scales already."

They all climbed out of the curtains and formed up in a long line. They held each other by the waist.

"One, two, three, GO!" said Mr Downes.

And they all began to dance after Mr Downes. In and out of the desks, weaving and coiling like a snake. The classroom wasn't big enough. So Mr Downes opened the door and they danced out into the corridor.

Halfway down, a door flew open. Mrs Maltby stood there.

"WHAT is going on?" she cried.

"I'm sorry," Mr Downes panted as he danced past her. "Just a small dragon. Nothing to worry about."

Next day Chris said to Steve. "There's got to be

fireworks. Tuan says it won't be the same without them."

"You can't buy fireworks in February," said Steve. "It's the wrong time of year."

"I couldn't buy them in November. They cost money," Chris said.

"Anyway, you're not old enough. They wouldn't sell them to you."

"I know where he keeps them though."

"Who?"

"Mr Bennett. He's got the paper shop next to Mr

Spiers' pet shop. There's a room at the back where he keeps all his Mars bars and stuff. He puts the fireworks back there after Guy Fawkes' night."

"He'll lock it up, though. You couldn't get in."

"Not at night. What do you think I am? Spiderman? I'll have to get in in the daytime, won't I? When the door's open."

"He'll see you."

"I'm working on it."

Next door, in the pet shop, was the Great Dane, Fred. Fred was the best guard dog in the city. Thieves took one look at his slobbering smile and kept their hands to themselves. But he had one weakness. Aniseed balls.

It was five past nine. All the people rushing to work had bought their newspapers and gone. The shops were quiet. Chris put his head round the door of the pet shop.

"Hello," said Mr Spiers. "Aren't you late for school?"

"Overslept," said Chris. "I'm on my way."

Mr Spiers went out to the back to get some more sacks of dog biscuits.

Chris held out his hand to Fred. In his palm was an aniseed ball. Fred bent his great head. Water dripped from his jaws. He followed Chris next door.

There were no customers in the paper shop. With his back to Mr Bennett, Chris put the open packet of aniseed balls on the sweet counter. Then he moved aside and started to look at the comics.

Suddenly there was a great roar from Mr Bennett.

"That dog! He's eating my sweets!"

Fred had put two huge paws on the counter. His jaws were tearing at the bag of aniseed balls. He was dribbling all over the chocolate bars and packets of sweets.

"Get off!"

Mr Bennett heaved at Fred's collar with both hands. Fred growled quietly and went on eating aniseed balls.

"I'm fetching your master! I'm not standing for this!"

And Mr Bennett disappeared next door. Quick as a rocket, Chris was round the counter and into the store-room at the back. The fireworks were on the top shelf. Up on a stool, snatch a box, under his coat, back into the shop.

Fred had dropped one of the aniseed balls on to the floor. Chris picked it up, dusted it off and put it in his mouth. Mr Spiers came running into the shop after Mr Bennett.

"Oh, dear!" he cried, "Fred! You naughty boy! Whatever made you do that?"

Fred wagged his tail and his dribble flew all over the shop.

"'Bye, Mr Bennett," said Chris hastily, and slipped out of the door.

The day of the dragon dance came. All Mr Downes' class were under the dragon. All except Tuan. Everyone in the school had dressed up. The fourth years had gongs and drums, and had to be stopped from making a noise too soon. The rest of the third year had coloured banners. The second year had made paper lanterns. And the first years had flags on sticks.

But there were no fireworks. And Tuan had said it wouldn't be a proper Chinese New Year without them.

Tuan stepped forward. He dipped a long paint-brush into a pot of paint and handed it to Mrs Maltby. She smiled at him.

"I've always wanted to do this! Come on, Tuan, let's do it together."

In front of the whole school, they painted the last white spot in the middle of the dragon's eye.

And, with a roar, Rahat made the dragon come to life. The gongs rang and the drums banged. The banners and flags waved, the lanterns bobbed. The dragon danced wildly round the playground. But there were no fireworks.

Then, "Excuse me!" said Chris, to the pair of legs in front of him.

He wriggled out of the dragon-skin, on the side away from the crowd, and disappeared round the corner of the building.

The bundle of fireworks was still where he had hidden it, wrapped in a plastic bag and stuffed into the gutter above the classroom window. Chris jumped down again and reached his hand into the bag. He drew out a banger. Then he felt in his pocket for the box of matches.

His heart sank. What a fool he was. Ever since that time with the hay-bale he had stopped carrying matches with him. He'd never thought to bring a box today.

He stared miserably down at the rockets, the Catherine wheels, the golden rain. He couldn't do anything right. He'd pinched the fireworks from Mr Bennett. He'd brought them into school, when it wasn't allowed. And still Tuan wouldn't get his fireworks. It had all been for nothing.

A familiar voice rasped over his head.

"And what are you up to *this* time?"

Then Mrs Maltby saw what he was holding. He heard her gasp.

"You . . . brought . . . fireworks . . . into . . . *school?*"

Chris didn't know where he got the courage from. He thrust the fireworks at Mrs Maltby. Things could hardly get worse, anyway.

"They're not for me. They're for Tuan. Honest, Miss. He says it won't be a proper New Year without them. Would *you* let them off for us, Miss? Go on! Please!"

For a moment he held his breath, waiting for her to explode. Then, to his amazement, her face changed. She started to *laugh*. She looked almost human.

"Well, it's my own fault! I should have thought of it myself. Here! Give them to me before we have another accident!"

She marched across the playground.

"Mr Downes. Matches!"

She stuck the stick of a rocket firmly into the flowerbed, lit the blue paper and stepped well back. The dragon stopped dancing. Some heads peeped out from under the skin to watch.

Afterwards, Chris was never quite sure what happened next. The rocket started to smoke. It sizzled. Then, at the last moment, the stick seemed to bend and sag. With a piercing whine the rocket shot across the playground and buried itself in the roof of the bicycle shed. There was a brief silence, then a violent exlosion of blue and purple sparks. A little yellow flame ran up the roof and began to climb the wall.

Half the dragon legs, who hadn't seen what was happening, leaped into the air in surprise, and the other half fell over on to the playground. The first years screamed. Tuan jumped up and down in excitement, clapping his hands.

"Crumbs!" gasped Chris. "She's set fire to the school!"

Steve threw the dragon's tail off him.

"Can I smash the fire alarm?" he cried. "Can I?"

And before anyone could stop him, he dashed into school and broke the glass. The alarm bell rang out deafeningly, but nobody came out of the building because everyone was in the playground already. Mr Downes sprinted into the office and dialled 999.

But Mrs Maltby was quicker than any of them. She seized a fire-extinguisher and rushed into the smoke. Foam hissed on the hot roof.

From the end of the street, a siren blared. A

fire-engine screeched to a halt outside the gate. Mums, dads and grandparents rushed into the street to see what was happening. Firemen in yellow leggings jumped down and raced across the playground, unrolling their hose as they came. The front half of the dragon leaped out of the way. But the back half ran in the wrong direction and fell over the hosepipe. Now the pipe was writhing and wriggling as the water came pumping along it, so that it was like a live serpent fighting with the dragon.

"Line up in your classes!" yelled Mr Downes. But nobody heard him.

Mrs Maltby turned, black-faced and triumphant, and waved her extinguisher at the fire-officer.

"Quite unnecessary!" she said. "I've put it out myself. Just a little dragon that got out of control."

Then the water came gushing out of the hosepipe, drenching her and all the second years and the paper lanterns. Steam rose from the roof.

"Sorry, Ma'am!" apologised the fire-officer. "But I think you'll find your fire's out *now*."

Next moment, Rahat, wearing the dragon's head, seized him by the hand.

"Happy New Year!" she cried.

And before he knew what was happening, the dragon was dancing him across the playground, with

all the firemen in their helmets and yellow trousers joining in. The gongs rang and the drums banged. Tuan grabbed Mrs Maltby by one hand and Mr Downes by the other and danced them in front of the dragon's head, while the mums and dads and grandparents clapped and cheered.

Chris leaned weakly against Steve's shoulder.

"I don't believe it. She warned me dragons breathed fire. I didn't think she really meant it!"